7/21

INSPIRED BY THE LIFE AND LYRICS OF DAVID BOWIE

# STARBOY

## JAMI GIGOT

Henry Holt and Company
New York

FROM A LITTLE ROOM in a small brick house on a quiet London street, David stared up at the starry sky.

"Is anybody out there?" he whispered.

For as long as David
could remember, he'd
felt like a stranger on
his own planet.

As if he'd fallen to
Earth from outer space.

He had mismatched eyes; long, spindly legs made for dancing;

and sticky-out ears with a special knack for catching noises no one else seemed to hear.

So special that when
he listened closely,
David could detect a
faint cosmic murmur.

A chattering of stars.

When David heard this star chatter, his entire body would vibrate with far-out energy.

His eyes would FLASH.

His legs would SHIMMY-SHAKE,

and all ten toes would TIP-TAP.

As David danced, he felt connected to
the universe and the rhythm of the stars.

If only he could share this feeling with someone else.

At school, David could not sit still.
He TIP-TAPPED down the halls,

and SHIMMY-SHAKED in class.

He added a FLASH of color wherever
he went and let his imagination run wild.

But some of the kids didn't feel the same rhythm. They thought David was strange.

"What planet are you from?"
they asked, laughing.

*I wish I knew,* thought David.

He trudged back into class,
falling in line with everyone else.

That night, alone in his room, David's body
began to hum with rhythm again.

A spark began to flicker inside him . . .

But he was tired.
Lonely.
So David shut the window.
Let the spark fade out.

He couldn't hear the stars
chattering anymore.

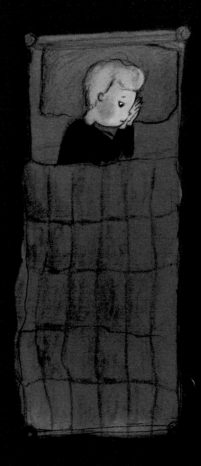

But something didn't feel right.

It was quiet.

Too quiet.

Then a hum started.
A soft, whispering tone . . .

Suddenly, there was a crackle. A SPARKLE!

The radio on David's windowsill burst to life.
Music flooded David's room.
It was EXTRAORDINARY!

With the rhythm of the stars,
joy tickled through him in waves.
The star chatter would never leave him.
It was a part of him.

"I hear you!" he shouted happily.

# "I HEAR YOU!"

David felt like himself again.

The rhythm rolled through David like electricity. He rushed around the house, gathering whatever he could find to keep the music going.

An old pot.

A pair of spoons.

A tin can.

He tapped a wooden crate and tied a string to a broomstick and plucked.

YES, THAT WAS IT!

By the light of the moon, he rocked to the beat of the stars.

In the morning, he raced to school.
He couldn't wait to share his discovery.

Even in daylight,

David felt the rhythm of the stars humming inside him.

He plucked out the chords, blared the horn, and banged to the beat.

As the star chatter hummed
loudly, his imagination ran wild.
He was a pirate, a duke,
an astronaut, a goblin king!

Commotion and color
swirled around him.
Rhythms and riffs, like the
hearts of stars beating
loudly, began to spread . . .

When David opened his eyes, everyone was tip-tapping and shimmy-shaking to the rhythm.

The star energy was moving them, too!

David smiled.
The spark inside him
radiated like a shining star.

# A NOTE FROM THE AUTHOR/ILLUSTRATOR

Although my book tells the fantastical tale of a boy's communication with the stars, it was inspired by the real life and lyrics of David Bowie, one of the most original and influential musicians of our time. I've been a huge fan of his for many years, and as I delved into the story of David's life, I felt compelled to write a fictional narrative rather than a straight biography. I wanted to focus on his imaginative personality, what he might have felt like as a child, and ultimately how he came to fearlessly express himself. And I wanted to encapsulate this in an unusual and interesting way, an homage of sorts to David Bowie's own unique character.

Born David Robert Jones in London in 1947, David Bowie was involved in music from a very young age. As a teenager, he began playing in skiffle bands, musical jam sessions where the musicians would use homemade or improvised instruments. He would pluck out rhythms on a tea-chest bass (an instrument made from a wooden crate, a broomstick, and a string), and soon he taught himself ukulele, and begged his father for a saxophone (which David paid back by working a part-time delivery job).

When David was a child, the musical landscape was rapidly changing as music became more energetic, with a faster pace. Rhythm and blues was evolving into rock 'n' roll, and David was strongly influenced by American musicians like Little Richard, Fats Domino, and Elvis Presley. He was also turned on to jazz by his older half brother Terry, who introduced him to John Coltrane and Charles Mingus. By the age of fifteen, he was playing in his first rock 'n' roll band.

David had a relentless impulse to create. As he began discovering his own voice and sound, he was also inspired by theater and fashion, and studied dramatic arts at the London Dance Centre. David began experimenting with his performances in revolutionary ways, combining music with theater, dance, poetry, and even mime. He wore flamboyant costumes, including a long silk dress, a bright neon-striped suit with shoulder pads and red platform boots, a polka-dot scarf and an eye patch.

David moved chameleon-like through different career phases, never following trends, but creating them. He invented various personas, from the fantastical orange-haired, alien rock star Ziggy Stardust to the glittery Aladdin Sane with the iconic zigzag painted on his forehead, to the lean and sleek, suit-wearing Thin White Duke. Indeed, he was a musical revolution and an avid creator, producing twenty-seven studio albums, performing in twenty-seven films, and releasing over one hundred singles during his career.

Although David Bowie achieved great fame and success, he suffered personal hardships. Mental illness ran in his family, and several family members—including his beloved half brother Terry—spent their lives struggling with a disorder called schizophrenia. This affected David tremendously and he worried about his own mental health. Music and art became an outlet to explore his fears, with "subject matter based around loneliness, coupled with isolation, some kind of spiritual search, and a looking for a way into communicating with other people."

David ultimately did find a way to communicate. Through his art, he reached the hearts and minds of people all over the world and encouraged them to express themselves, assuring them that no matter how different or weird they may feel, they were not alone.

David Bowie died on January 10, 2016, two days after the release of his final album, *Blackstar*. His legacy still inspires musicians and artists across generations. David Bowie was an otherworldly talent, and we are lucky to have had him on planet Earth, if only for a short while.

"David Bowie: Verbatim," produced by Ten Alps, BBC Radio 4, London, January 30, 2016.

# FACTS ABOUT DAVID BOWIE

★ David Bowie was born David Robert Jones, but changed his last name to Bowie (after the Bowie knife) to avoid confusion with another big pop star of that time, Davy Jones of the Monkees.

★ Although I have exaggerated his distinctive eyes in my artwork, David did have a condition called anisocoria, in which a person's eyes have different-size pupils, and it can make eyes appear to be different in color. When he was fifteen, he got into a fight with his friend George Underwood over a girl, and his eye was permanently damaged. The two remained lifelong friends, and David later thanked George for giving him "a kind of mystique."

★ At seventeen, David founded the Society for the Prevention of Cruelty to Long-Haired Men.

★ When the crew of Apollo 11 landed on the moon on July 20, 1969, David's song "Space Oddity" was played during the BBC news program's coverage of the historic event. It was an instant sensation in the United Kingdom and became his first hit single.

★ David was also a talented actor. His most well-known roles were Jareth the Goblin King in the 1986 movie *Labyrinth* and the alien Thomas Jerome Newton in the 1976 film *The Man Who Fell to Earth*.

★ A constellation, consisting of seven stars that shine in the shape of a lightning bolt, is named in David's honor. Can you spot it in the book?

★ There is a spider named *Heteropoda davidbowie*, in tribute to David's album *Ziggy Stardust and the Spiders from Mars*. The spider is not from Mars but does have wild, bright orange hair.

★ To date, David Bowie has sold over 140 million records.

★ In 2013, Canadian astronaut Chris Hadfield performed "Space Oddity" on board the International Space Station. It was the first-ever music video performed in outer space.

# SOURCES

Buckley, David. *Strange Fascination: David Bowie: The Definitive Story* (revised ed.). London: Virgin Books, 2001.

"David Bowie." *Tonight*. London: BBC, November 24, 1964.

"David Bowie: Verbatim." Produced by Ten Alps. London: BBC Radio 4, January 30, 2016.

Hadfield, Chris. "Space Oddity." Uploaded by Rare Earth. *YouTube*, May 13, 2013.

Hou, Kathy and Iman. "Iman on Wellness, Diversity, and Turning 60." *The Cut*, July 23, 2015.

Kirk, Ashley. "David Bowie: The Legendary Singer in Numbers." *The Daily Telegraph* (London), January 11, 2016.

Kreps, Daniel. "Belgian Astronomers Pay Tribute to David Bowie with New Constellation." *Rolling Stone*, January 16, 2016.

"Rare Yellow Spider Named After David Bowie." *The Telegraph* (London), September 7, 2009.

Sandford, Christopher. *Bowie: Loving the Alien* (revised ed.). Boston: Da Capo Press, 2009

Thompson, Jody. "Sixty Things about David Bowie." *BBC News*, January 8, 2007.

Trynka, Paul. *David Bowie: Starman*. New York: Little, Brown and Company, 2011.

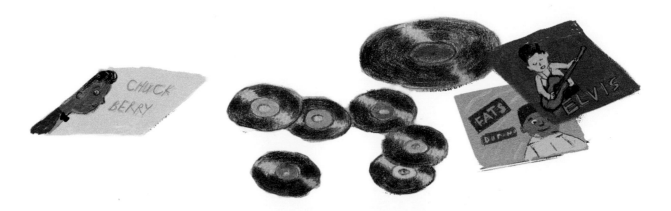

*To the kooks, rebels, and heroes of the world.*

*And with heartfelt thanks to Tiffany Liao and Wendi Gu.*

*—J. G.*

Henry Holt and Company, *Publishers since 1866*

Henry Holt® is a registered trademark of Macmillan Publishing Group, LLC

120 Broadway, New York, NY 10271 • mackids.com

Copyright © 2021 by Jami Gigot. All rights reserved.

Our books may be purchased in bulk for promotional, educational, or business use. Please
contact your local bookseller or the Macmillan Corporate and Premium Sales Department at
(800) 221-7945 ext. 5442 or by email at MacmillanSpecialMarkets@macmillan.com.

Library of Congress Control Number: 2020919584

First Edition, 2021

Book design by Cindy De la Cruz

Printed in China by RR Donnelley Asia Printing Solutions Ltd.,

Dongguan City, Guangdong Province

ISBN 978-1-250-23943-3

1  3  5  7  9  10  8  6  4  2